PROLOGUE
VALENTINA

I was sold like property on the day of my father's funeral. I'd thought his death would set me free, but I'd never really understood what it meant to have all my freedoms stripped away. Until that day, I'd been living in a child's fantasy.

At the funeral, my eyes were dry. I didn't shed any tears over Antonio Moreno because I had none to offer him. I did my best to arrange my features into something sorrowful, but if anything, I felt relief. I'd never tremble in his shadow again.

He certainly didn't loom large now. Not laying out in his coffin, his eyes closed but his granite jaw as hard and forbidding as ever. Despite the harsh set of his face in death, I realized for the first time that my father was actually a short man. Even though he'd been half a foot taller than me, I was only fourteen and still growing.

It was strange, looking at his coffin and realizing

that he'd never been nearly as big as I'd thought. It was almost funny.

I pressed my lips together to keep them from curving up in amusement. I shouldn't be smiling. Even if I held no love for my distant, intimidating father, my grandmother would switch me for mocking the dead. She'd do it out of love, but she'd switch me all the same. *Abuela* rarely disciplined me, but she was raising me to be a good, honest girl, and I wouldn't let her down. Especially not in front of all the strange, scary men who were attending my father's funeral.

Andrés' hand covered mine in a silent show of support. I glanced over at my brother where he sat in the church pew beside me. He might be my half-brother by technical terms, but he was the person I was closest to in the world. We shared a father, and we shared the same opinion of him: that he was a callous, ruthless man.

When Andrés' dark chocolate eyes met mine, I noticed the relief that shone from them. I wasn't the only one who wouldn't miss our father. I squeezed my brother's hand and allowed a small smile to play around my mouth. Others would see the gesture as a sister comforting her older sibling, but in reality, we were sharing a private moment of joy. We were free.

I swallowed a yelp when pain flared on my left thigh. I knew better than to cry when Cristian hurt me. I tore my eyes from Andrés, but I didn't dare look at Cristian, my other half-brother and my own personal demon. He was nothing like Andrés.

Then again, as the oldest son and heir to my father's cocaine empire, Cristian had been subject to his full, cruel attention for his entire life.

I wished *Abuela* were sitting beside me instead of Cristian, but he hadn't even allowed her in the same pew. Since she wasn't father's blood relative, she wasn't supposed to sit at the front of the church.

I just prayed that Cristian would leave us all alone at our little house on the corner of our father's estate once we returned home.

No. Not *our father's estate*. It was Cristian's now. He might only be twenty, but father had left him everything. The same hour Antonio had died from his heart attack, Cristian had begun consolidating his power and securing his position. He was young, so there would be challenges to his control, probably by many of the dangerous men who filled this church, pretending to mourn.

The fake mourners were processing down the aisle, taking their turn to say a prayer—or a silent curse—over Antonio's body. I watched them instead of peeking over at Cristian. It was safer that way.

Or so I thought, until an older man in a tailored black suit turned away from the coffin, and his dark eyes caught mine. His cheekbones were defined, his cheeks hollow. His narrow jaw tapered to a sharp point, which was emphasized by his thin black beard. I recognized Vicente Rodríguez from my father's lavish parties. I'd become adept at memorizing important names and faces at a young age, and Vicente was one of Antonio's most powerful friends.

But the line between friend and enemy was thin in our world, and the way Vicente's lip curled at Cristian made unease stir in my gut. I might not like my half-brother, but if he was killed, I wouldn't have a home on the family estate anymore. I'd be homeless, penniless. Cristian's success meant stability for Andrés and me, so even though I didn't like him, I was on big brother's side.

Vicente's eyes left Cristian, and his gaze fell on me. He took a few lingering seconds to study my face. Then, his eyes lowered, and he wasn't studying my face. I shifted against the wooden pew, becoming very aware of the fact that my breasts had grown over the months since I'd last seen him. My black dress was modest, but the way he looked at my body wasn't.

He wasn't the only one looking. When my eyes skipped past him, no longer able to bear the connection, I found another man watching me. His eyes were black, bottomless. His face was doughy, but his shoulders were broad. I wasn't as familiar with this stocky man who flanked Vicente, but I was fairly certain that his name was Hugo. He'd never been far from Vicente's side when I'd seen him in the past.

Now, they were both looking at me. Both studying my developing body.

My stomach churned, and my face burned with shame.

Andrés' hand tightened on mine like a vise, and I heard a low, angry sound rumble from his chest. Luckily, the organ music was loud enough to smother the aggressive noise. I wasn't sure what would happen if Andrés snapped at Vicente and his friend, but it wouldn't be anything good.

Within moments, Vicente and Hugo finished walking past us to take their places farther back in the church. I heaved in a sharp breath, and I squeezed Andrés' hand tighter to hide my trembling fingers.

The funeral went by in a haze after that. My skin continued to crawl where the men had looked at me, and my hand grew slick and sweaty against Andrés'. He didn't seem to mind; he didn't pull away.

All I could think about was getting back home and changing out of this dress, which now felt far too form-fitting and sophisticated for my age. I wanted to sit at grandmother's kitchen table and eat *arroz con leche* in my pajamas before watching a telenovela. Andrés pretended he didn't like them, but he always sat beside me on the couch and watched the drama unfold. Maybe we'd play a game of chess, too. Spending time with my best friend and my grandmother would calm my nerves.

"Valentina," *Abuela* said my name in an urgent tone. "Get dressed."

"What?" I asked thickly. I'd dozed off on the sofa, comfy in my pajamas, my belly full of dessert. I blinked the sleep from my eyes and glanced at the window. The curtains were drawn, but I could tell it was dark outside. *Abuela* should be telling me to get in bed, not to get dressed.

"What's going on?" Andrés asked. He was lounging on the couch beside me, still in his suit from the funeral. It was rumpled from lazing around for hours in front of the TV. We never had gotten to play chess, but I'd been too emotionally exhausted for a game against my wickedly smart brother, anyway.

"Cristian wants to see Valentina," *Abuela* said. Her tanned, weathered face was drawn with worry, her wrinkles deeper than I'd ever seen them. I'd never really noticed her age before, but now, her gray hair looked wiry around her cheeks, and the lines at the corners of her lips appeared carved into her skin.

I sat up quickly, the fog of sleep clearing from my mind. "Why does he want to see me? What time is it?"

"Nearly midnight. I don't know why, but he called to say he's on his way. He'll be here in a few minutes. You need to get dressed."

"He's coming here?" Fear knifed through me, but I started moving to obey my grandmother. I darted into the bedroom and grabbed the first thing I found in my drawer—jeans and a t-shirt with happy little cartoon monkeys on it.

Cristian never came to our house. He stayed in the big house, with our father.

But now, father was dead. This was Cristian's domain: the entire estate. He could come and go as he pleased.

As I hurried back out into the living room, I heard the front door open without so much as a knock to request entry.

"What do you want?" Andrés challenged.

I hurried to his side and grabbed his hand, silently urging him not to antagonize our sadistic older brother.

Cristian entered the living room. He wasn't alone.

Vicente Rodríguez and his stocky friend, Hugo, followed my oldest brother into our house, invading our safe space.

I immediately took a step back, seeking shelter behind Andrés. Their eyes were on me again, dark and hungry. Vicente's gaze dropped to my t-shirt, lingered. I realized I hadn't put on a bra. I still wasn't used to hiding my nipples, and now they peaked against the soft material.

He frowned. "She's younger than I thought."

"Does that matter?" Hugo drawled.

Vicente's eyes left me to fix on my grandmother. "Is she a woman yet?"

"She's a child," *Abuela* replied, her voice shaking. She

stepped up to stand beside Andrés, further shielding me.

"You know what I mean," Vicente pressed, his tone ice cold.

I didn't know what he meant. Of course I wasn't a woman. I was fourteen.

"She's a child," *Abuela* repeated, her own tone hardening.

I peeked around her shoulder, so I could study the scary men. I had to know what was happening.

"She'll be a woman soon enough," Cristian said, addressing Vicente. He wasn't even glancing in my direction. "She already looks like one. Do we have a deal or not?"

"What deal?" Andrés demanded. "What are you talking about?"

Cristian's black gaze turned on him, pinning him in place. His lips curved with malice. "Father left me with a few debts. Mr. Rodríguez has generously offered to forgive those debts. For a small price."

"Get out," *Abuela* seethed, her tanned skin going red. "Get the fuck out of my house." I'd never heard her curse before. It made my pulse spike and my palms sweat.

"This is *my* house," Cristian drawled. "And you'll be lucky if I allow you to stay here when she's gone."

She? Who was Cristian talking about?

His dark eyes found mine, and my heart dropped. In

that moment, I knew. I couldn't hide behind a child's ignorance.

It's me. I'm the price he's paying.

The cold way he regarded me told me he thought he was getting the better end of the deal than Vicente.

Andrés seemed to understand at the same time, because he launched himself at Cristian with a furious roar.

My beloved brother might be big, but Cristian was older. Crueler. More practiced at hurting people.

Abuela shrieked when Cristian's fist slammed into Andrés' gut. She wrapped her arms around me in a protective gesture, but Hugo was already moving toward us. Andrés dropped to his knees, and Cristian punched him hard across the jaw. I screamed as blood sprayed from his lips. He dropped to the hardwood floor. He didn't get up.

Cristian didn't seem to care that Andrés had been subdued. He drove his boot into my sweet brother's ribs again and again. Andrés moaned and curled in on himself.

I struggled against my grandmother's hold. I had to get to Cristian and make him stop hurting Andrés.

I couldn't have freed myself from her desperate grip by my own strength, but Hugo grabbed her arm and ripped her away from me. Cold air closed around me, freezing me in place for a moment. I was alone, completely unprotected. And the people I loved were being hurt. I couldn't go to both of them at the same time, and my hesitation cost me the chance to get to either of them.

Vicente's hand closed around my wrist. "Let's go, *chiquita*."

I screamed and lashed out. I'd never fought anyone in my life, but my fist swung toward his face. It glanced off his jaw, seeming to cause him no harm at all.

Instead, my defiant action incited rage. His eyes flashed, and I had a moment to register his fist drawing back before pain exploded through my skull. The world flickered around me.

I felt my body being lifted up, trapped against a strong chest. The movement made the pain spike. I registered one last moment of terror before I fell into darkness.

CHAPTER 1
VALENTINA

My head throbbed, and my mouth was dry. I'd been awake for a while, drifting in and out of awareness, but I hadn't dared to open my eyes. I couldn't face reality. It was easier to sink into the pain in my head than to think about the fact that I'd been ripped away from my home and my family.

Hot tears slipped from beneath my closed eyelids to fall down my cheeks. I couldn't drift in pain and exhaustion anymore. The soft illumination through my lids let me know that night had passed. The sun was rising, rousing me.

I became more aware of my essential needs. I was desperate for water, and I needed to go to the bathroom.

I peeled my eyes open, wincing against the wash of morning light.

I didn't have time to really study my surroundings; my needs were too insistent. Spotting a sink and tiled floor through an open door across the room from me, I quickly got out of the unfamiliar bed and rushed into the bathroom.

My hasty movements made my head ache, but I almost welcomed the discomfort. It gave me something to focus on. If I was preoccupied by my physical distress, I could put off the moment when I'd have to fully contemplate my situation.

I saw to my most pressing urges before going to the sink for water. A small glass on the counter served me better than cupped hands, and I gratefully filled it. The cooling liquid relieved my parched tongue.

Once I'd drained the glass, I noted that a new, packaged toothbrush waited for me on the counter, as well as a fresh tube of toothpaste. Moving on autopilot, I brushed my teeth, feeling moderately better when my mouth was minty fresh and no longer dry.

I finally took a moment to really look at my reflection in the mirror. My black hair was wild around my face, my tanned cheeks paler than usual. A bruise darkened my jaw. It was purple and ugly, marring my face with violence. Cristian had left bruises on my body in the past, but he'd never touched my face. The shock of the vicious mark made my chest tighten. While I knew it would fade, the sight made tears pool in my brown eyes. The warm droplets caught in my thick lashes as I struggled to blink them back. I took a deep breath, but it hitched in my throat. When I exhaled, the air left my chest on a harsh sob.

My legs trembled, and I didn't bother trying to fight off my impending emotional breakdown for a second longer. My knees folded, and I sank down onto the cool tiles beneath me, curling up on my side as sobs wracked my body.

I was in a strange room in a strange house, trapped with strange men who had taken me from my home and my family.

I remembered Vicente's thin lips curled in a sneer as he struck my face; Hugo's cruel black eyes narrowed as he tore *Abuela* away from me; Cristian's sick, satisfied smile as he kicked Andrés over and over again.

Abuela. Andrés.

I longed for the warmth of their comforting arms around me, but I was utterly alone.

I hugged my own arms more tightly around my chest, as though the child-like position could protect me from reality.

"Shut up."

I jolted at the low, growled words. The boy's pale green eyes glowered at me from above; the soft morning light caught in them, making them glow. I had a brief impression of a panther, a predator staring me down. I was small and broken beneath him. Easy prey.

I curled up more tightly, fearing he'd lash out and kick me the way Christian had beat Andrés. The way the boy's full lips sneered at me warned me of impending violence.

I sniffled, but my sob caught in my chest. I didn't want to anger him further, and he'd told me to shut up.

"Stop crying," he commanded, his harshly square jaw tightening.

I blinked hard, but I couldn't stop the tears from falling. My breath hitched in my throat as I suppressed another sob. I stared up at him, fear making me tremble. My fingers began to go numb, and I realized I'd laced them tightly together in front of my knees.

"Do you know what time it is?" he demanded. "You woke me up."

"I'm sorry," I choked out.

"Who the hell are you, anyway? What are you doing in my house?"

"I'm Valentina," I squeaked out my name. "Vicente..." I tried not to gag around the acid words. "I was brought here." A shudder raced through my body. "I'm sorry I woke you up." I apologized to the stranger because I didn't want him to hurt me.

The boy's chin tilted, and his pale green eyes seemed to scan through me, studying me. "Fine," he snapped after several tense seconds of heavy silence. "Just be quiet. I'm going back to sleep for an hour."

I nodded, my cheek brushing over the cool tiles. I hadn't stood to face the boy, and he seemed unconcerned by my distressed position on the floor. He was as callous as Cristian, and I didn't dare provoke him.

Only when he'd stomped out of the bedroom and snapped the door shut behind him did I gasp in a shuddering breath. I suppressed another sob on the exhale. I didn't want the boy to return. I didn't want him to hurt me. I'd been ripped from the safe haven of my home and taken into a strange, violent world. The cruelty of the men who'd taken me had proven that much.

Is she a woman yet? Vicente's puzzling words echoed through my head. I wasn't sure exactly what he'd meant, but my grandmother's incensed response let me know it was nothing good.

I remembered the way he'd studied my body at the funeral, and I shuddered. I had a terrible suspicion what he'd meant, but I chose to cling to innocent ignorance.

She's a child, Grandmother had said.

I'm just a girl, I told myself. My body might be developing in ways I didn't fully understand, but I couldn't imagine being considered a woman at my age. Women were much older. Twenty, at least.

I'd never known my mother—she died giving birth to me—but my father had taken enough mistresses for me to know I was nothing like the sultry, sophisticated women who'd lived in the big house, no matter how quickly they'd come and gone.

I took several deep breaths to calm my fearful trembling. I couldn't stay curled up on the bathroom tiles forever, and the cool surface was causing ice to sink into my bones.

Slowly, I pushed myself up, my head spinning

slightly from the lingering effects of my injury. I closed my eyes and waited for the dizziness to pass before rising from my kneeling position and getting to my feet.

I was too fearful of the boy to leave the bedroom. I didn't want to disturb him again.

Despite my situation, there was a small sense of security in the solitude of the bedroom. No one was here to hurt me.

Yet.

The room was much nicer than my bedroom in our modest house on father's estate. But the huge, canopied bed and heavy, red velvet drapes framing a large arched window left me cold. The room might be spacious, but it was far too mature for me. My bedroom back home had been painted in soft shades of pink, and cheery little monkeys—my favorite animal—had cuddled me to sleep, decorating my blankets.

I longed for the comfort of Jorge, my plush monkey who kept me company every night. Andrés teased me about him sometimes, telling me I was too old to sleep with a stuffed animal. But Jorge was like a friend to me, and I'd whispered my secrets to him in the night.

Like the fact that I missed my mother, even though I'd never known her. I'd told him how I feared my father and Cristian. I wouldn't admit it to anyone else. *Abuela* provided a home for Andrés and me, and I didn't want her to think I didn't love her. I didn't want her to think I sometimes wished I had loving parents, too.

Tears stung the corners of my eyes again, and I hastily blinked them back.

Stop crying, the boy had ordered.

Seeking the only comfort I could think of, I got back in bed and tugged the covers over my head, as though I could hide from the monsters that likely lurked in this unfamiliar house.

What are you doing in my house? The boy was definitely one of those monsters, and he lived here. He was close enough that he'd heard me crying.

I shivered at the idea of his nearness, and I burrowed deeper into the covers.

I wasn't sure how long I lay there, trying to quiet my distressed thoughts. After a while, I heard the bedroom door open. I sank farther into the mattress, cowering from the stranger.

"Valentina," a feminine voice called softly. "You need to wake up. We're having breakfast soon."

I didn't emerge from the covers. I didn't want to leave the relative safety of the bedroom, and I didn't know this woman; another stranger who might hurt me.

"Valentina," she said, more sharply. "Get up."

"I don't want to," I whispered.

She sighed. "Don't make me come over there." The warning didn't hold any venom, but it was a warning, nonetheless.

With trembling fingers, I pulled the covers down, poking my head out to peer at the woman. "Who are you?" I asked, my voice small.

Her pouty red lips pressed together, her delicate, tanned features souring as her brown eyes narrowed. "I told you to get up. Don't test me."

I swung my legs over the side of the bed and willed my shaking knees to support me as I stood. The woman eyed me up and down, examining me. She lingered on my monkey t-shirt, and I hugged my arms around me to hide my breasts. I didn't like when people looked at them. It made my cheeks burn and my stomach drop.

The woman's perfectly painted lips twisted downward, but the frown didn't diminish her beautiful features.

"You are young," she murmured, as though speaking to herself. She sighed again. "My name is Mariana. Come on. I'm supposed to help you get ready today."

Hesitantly, I walked toward where she beckoned to the bathroom. As I approached, I realized she was a petite woman. She was barely taller than my five-foot four frame, but the way her tight green wrap dress hugged her curves couldn't have made the age difference between us more obvious. Her eyes were framed by dark lashes, which were so thick that the effect could only be achieved with makeup.

I noted that she was perfectly polished, from her red lipstick to her crimson-lacquered fingernails. It seemed odd that she was so put together at this time of day, as though she was ready to go to one of my father's dinner parties. Only, we were getting ready for breakfast. Despite her makeup, she was obviously a natural beauty, with a heart-shaped face and slender, straight nose. Her tanned cheeks seemed to practically glow.

I couldn't discern her age, but she was definitely a woman. I felt awkward and disheveled beside her. Were all women this made up in the morning? I didn't have a frame of reference other than *Abuela*, and I'd never seen her wear any trace of makeup.

My familiar longing for a mother tightened my chest. *Abuela* loved me, but she'd never taught me anything about becoming a woman. Maybe if I had a mother, I'd be a little more prepared to face Mariana.

As it was, I dropped my eyes and skirted around her into the bathroom.

"Take a shower," she ordered, but the command was softened by her sultry voice. "I have something you can wear. We'll get you clothes of your own later today, but we're close enough to the same size that you can wear something of mine."

The idea of wearing the beautiful woman's clothes made unease stir in my gut.

Is she a woman yet?

I shied away from the memory of Vicente's strange question. I didn't want to contemplate it.

"Hurry up," Mariana urged as she closed the bathroom door behind me.

Goosebumps erupted on my arms when I stripped off my shirt. Even though I was alone, I felt exposed in this unfamiliar place. The bathroom was opulent, with black and white checked tiles and a huge bathtub I could practically swim in.

I usually took a bath in the evening, but I'd been told to shower this morning. It went against my routine, but I felt dirty enough that stepping under the warm spray was a relief. I scrubbed at my body, vaguely noting the pretty scent of the lavender soap. Under other circumstances, I might have marveled at the sophisticated splendor of this bathroom. It was just as nice as the ones in the big house on my father's estate, but I'd never been allowed to spend the night there. Sometimes, when I'd allowed myself to imagine that my father was a kind man, I'd wished he'd invite me to stay and tuck me into bed at night.

But father was cruel and cold. He'd rarely spared me more than a passing glance and a sneer. He'd made it clear that he had no use for a daughter, especially not one conceived out of wedlock. My mother had been nothing more to him than a mistress, and he'd claimed that he only allowed *Abuela* and me to stay on the estate because I was his blood. And nothing more.

Now, I wasn't even allowed to remain in the modest home he'd granted me. Cristian had sold me, and I might never see home again.

My hot tears mingled with the warm water streaming down my cheeks, and I sniffled.

A sharp knock on the door snapped me out of my mounting grief and panic.

"Valentina. Hurry up. I need to get you ready for

breakfast," Mariana's voice penetrated the door, sharp with disapproval.

I didn't understand why I needed her to help me get ready. I was perfectly capable of brushing my hair and dressing myself.

But I was too intimidated to question her, so I turned off the shower and found a fluffy white towel to wrap around my body. I'd only just managed to cover myself when Mariana entered the bathroom without bothering to knock again.

I tucked the towel tightly in place around me, uncomfortable with so little fabric to shield my body from a stranger.

She seemed unconcerned by my discomfiture, and she breezed past me to the vanity. Opening a cabinet beneath the sink, she retrieved a round brush and hair dryer. I didn't usually use one, even though it could take hours for my thick waves to fully dry. My wet hair never bothered *Abuela* or Andrés. It was another feminine habit I'd never picked up.

"Come on," Mariana urged me closer. "It's not going to burn you."

She plugged in the hair dryer, and I stepped in front of the mirror. I couldn't look at my unusually pale cheeks and wide eyes. Instead, I focused on Mariana's lovely reflection as she began to run the brush through my hair. The bristles tickled my scalp, and the dryer warmed my skin. It wasn't an unpleasant sensation. If anything, the tug of the brush through my hair was slightly soothing, and some of my nerves calmed.

Was this what it felt like to have a mother? To be taken care of and shown how to behave like a woman?

Despite the warmth of the dryer on my head, my body flushed cold. This woman wasn't here to help me. Whatever her role, I couldn't mistake this strange interaction for maternal kindness. She was one of the monsters that lived in this house, and I wouldn't forget that, no matter how gently she was brushing my hair.

When she finished, my locks were glossy and sleek around my face, gently curled at the ends. My hair was much straighter than usual, making it fall longer, around my breasts.

I cursed their existence. I didn't want them. I didn't want people looking at them.

Petulant anger surged through me, and I flipped my hair behind my shoulders.

"Stop that," Mariana reprimanded. She rearranged my hair back into place.

I reached up to move it behind my shoulders again, but my defiance was quashed on a yelp when she smacked the back of my hand with the hairbrush.

"We have to be at the table in twenty minutes," she told me tersely. "Behave."

She put the dryer and brush back into their place beneath the sink and disappeared into the bedroom for a moment before returning with a pretty dress. I hadn't noticed it when she'd first entered the bedroom, but then again, I'd been hiding under the covers.

The dress was frilly and feminine, with pretty white flowers standing in contrast to the silky black fabric.

"We'll have to get you some bras and underwear," Mariana noted. "But this should cover you well enough for breakfast."

To my relief, she didn't make me drop my towel. Instead, she tugged the dress over my head, careful not to muss my newly-straightened hair. Once I was covered, she instructed me to pull the towel off. I let it slide to the floor, and she stepped behind me to fasten the zipper at the back of the dress.

To my surprise, it stuck a little at the middle of my upper back, the fabric straining over my chest. Again, I resented my breasts. They felt far too large. I'd barely been aware of them before father's funeral, but I was quickly growing to hate them.

The fabric was slightly loose around my waist, and it didn't quite hug my hips. Mariana tied the sash around the waist into a bow at my back.

Then, she went back into the bedroom, returning with a black plastic case. She set it on the countertop and unfastened it to reveal an array of makeup. I'd never seen so many lipsticks and rouges all together. My only frame of reference for makeup was what I'd seen on TV commercials and in magazines. Mariana's collection was bafflingly extensive. I didn't realize women needed so many products.

She stepped in front of me and studied my face for a moment before nodding slightly. She selected a compact and large makeup brush. The soft brush hairs against my cheeks felt even more soothing than the hairbrush, so I closed my eyes and focused on sensation for as long as possible, blocking out my confused thoughts and fears.

After a few minutes, she prompted me to open my eyes, so she could coat my lashes with mascara before painting my lips with a neutral lipstick.

Finally, she stepped back behind me, placing her hands on my shoulders as she studied my reflection in the mirror.

"Lovely," she approved.

I sucked in a gasp at my appearance. I hardly recognized the girl staring back at me, her dark lashes longer and thicker than ever and her lips looking far too full and pouty. The dress was as tight as I'd feared, straining over my chest before cinching in at my waist.

"Much better than that t-shirt," Mariana noted. "I'll make sure you get more pretty dresses like this. It suits you."

Tears welled in my eyes. I was in a strange house with a strange woman, and I was staring at a stranger in the mirror where my reflection should be.

"Don't cry," Mariana ordered. "You'll ruin your makeup."

The command was sharp enough that I blinked back my tears. The fear that had plagued me since I'd awoken rose up again, curling around my windpipe like a choking vine.

I remembered the cruel boy who'd snapped at me while I huddled on the floor, broken and sobbing.

Was he nearby? Would I see him again?

"Come on," Mariana urged. "We don't want to be late. Vicente doesn't like to be kept waiting."

I froze. I didn't want to see Vicente. My skin crawled when he looked at me.

Mariana took my hand and tugged me along in her wake, leading me out of the false safety of the bedroom and into the monsters' lair.

CHAPTER 2
VALENTINA

We strode down a long hallway, a crimson rug marking out path. Dark, hardwood floors were visible at either side, contrasting with the bright white walls. Those were adorned with paintings, intermittently interrupted by closed doorways to our right. To our left, large, arched windows allowed morning light to stream in and illuminate the house.

When we finally reached the end of the long hallway, a door was open before us. I hesitated, but Mariana took my hand and pulled me across the threshold. My palm was clammy against hers, but she seemed too intent on rushing me in to drop my hand.

"You're late." Vicente's cold drawl was soft, but it made menace roll through the room.

I stared at the mahogany table to avoid meeting his eye. Several dishes were covered with silver domes, keeping their contents warm. The spread was far more opulent than any breakfast table I'd ever seen.

Out of the corner of my eye, I noted Hugo seated to Vicente's right, and another, smaller figure beside him.

I tried to suppress my tremor. It was the boy who'd stared at me so coldly as I huddled on the bathroom floor.

Mariana didn't acknowledge my discomfiture. Instead, she pulled me along in her wake as she made her way to the head of the table and took her seat to Vicente's left. She indicated that I should sit beside her with a sharp tug on my hand.

I took a small, relieved breath when she finally released me, and I surreptitiously wiped my sweaty palm on the dress I'd been forced to wear.

I could feel the weight of their eyes on me, the press of their disapproval.

"I'm sorry we're late," Mariana said, her voice soft and deferential.

There was a moment of terrifying silence.

"Don't let it happen again." Vicente's tone was smooth, but it dripped with warning.

"Of course," Mariana promised. "I'll make sure she is on time from now on."

She?

They were talking about me. As though I wasn't even here. I felt more like an object than a person, and my skin crawled.

I fisted my hands in my lap to hide my shaking fingers and bit my lip to stop it from trembling.

I wouldn't cry again. Not after Mariana's warning not to ruin my mascara.

But more than that, I feared the boy who sat across the table from me.

Stop crying.

I didn't want to anger him with my tears.

Unable to help myself, I peeked up at him, primal imperatives telling me to assess the threat he posed.

His square jaw was tight, and his green eyes flared when my gaze met his. His attention fixed me in place, and I found that I couldn't look away as his eyes roved over my painted face before flicking down my body.

I squirmed in my seat, and his gaze immediately returned to my face. His full lips thinned to a harsh slash as he scowled at me.

I was finally able to break the connection when a man appeared at Vicente's side. He took one of the dishes from the table and uncovered it before serving Vicente a heaping portion of scrambled eggs, followed by fat sausages.

Vicente didn't so much as glance at him or thank him. Instead, he studied me, his eyes narrowed. At first, I thought the weight of his stare was one of disapproval because of my tardiness. After a few moments of his eyes lingering on my body, his head canting to the side, I realized he was studying me with a different intent.

My stomach twisted. I didn't understand why the

men wouldn't stop looking at me. All I knew was it made me feel queasy.

I stared at the table again, watching the man serve everyone's breakfast out of the corner of my eye. When he filled my plate, I nearly gagged at the rich scent of salted sausage. It wouldn't be possible for me to eat when nausea curled in my gut.

I glanced over at Mariana, trying to take my cues from her behavior. So far, she was the only person at this table who'd treated me with anything close to kindness. Despite my resentment of the way she'd styled my hair and dressed me up like a doll, I couldn't help seeking some sort of comfort from the older woman.

As she cut into her sausage, I noticed that she wasn't wearing a wedding band. A huge emerald adorned her finger, but nothing more. She clearly wasn't Vicente's wife, but she lived in his house and sat at his table.

I knew enough from my father's lifestyle to recognize that Mariana was Vicente's mistress. She was nothing more to him than a pretty companion.

Personally, I'd never really understood the point of mistresses. What purpose did they serve, other than lazing about the estate and looking beautiful? I did know that sometimes they got pregnant, but I didn't know how that happened. I'd seen my father kissing the women he kept around the house, just like the couples kissed in the telenovelas I watched. Those people were in love, whereas I'd never seen my father express affection for his mistresses.

I'd never really thought about these things before, but now, it seemed of vital importance. Mariana was Vicente's mistress, and she'd made me up to look like her. What did that mean for me?

A horrible vision of Vicente's thin lips pressed against my mouth made my stomach lurch. Over the last year, I'd become curious about kissing, about the love I saw expressed in my beloved TV shows.

The thought of sharing a kiss with the old man at the head of the table made me want to vomit.

"Eat your fucking food." I jolted at the snapped words, my gaze jumping to the angry boy who sat across from me. He glowered at me, his eyes flicking from my face to my untouched plate. Everyone else was finishing their breakfast, but I'd sat frozen as disgusting thoughts floated through my brain.

"Language, Adrián," Vicente drawled.

Suddenly, Hugo cuffed the boy hard on the back of his head. The boy—Adrián—winced, his eyes narrowing on me, as though it was my fault he'd been struck.

Mariana sighed. "If you don't eat now, you won't get anything until lunch," she warned me.

I shook my head, staring at the food cooling on my plate. "I can't," I said softly. "I don't feel good."

A moment of silence passed, and I felt everyone's eyes on me, pricking at my skin.

"She is young," Vicente finally said.

"Does it matter?" Hugo replied, a slight rasp to his tone. "Cristian was right. She looks like a woman."

"I'm not interested in deflowering a child," Vicente said coldly. "She can join Adrián in his studies until she's older."

"What?" Adrián burst out. "I don't want her around. I'm not going to be her fucking babysitter."

I heard the dull thud when Hugo struck him again for his filthy language, but I couldn't bring myself to look up at any of them. They were discussing my fate like I wasn't even a person. Like I had no free will.

I still didn't fully understand that I wasn't free anymore. This was my first day in my gilded cage.

CHAPTER 3
ADRIÁN

My tutor, Mrs. Gómez, droned on about algebra, addressing Valentina to assess her knowledge. It turned out, the girl had a tutor of her own at her former home, and she was actually quite advanced for her age.

She's fourteen, I reminded myself, tearing my gaze from her breasts, which strained against the silky dress she wore.

I'd thought she was a couple years older, closer to my age.

Then again, she was all made up now, her face painted and her hair sleekly styled. When I'd found her sobbing on the bathroom floor this morning, she'd appeared much younger. She'd looked like a scared little girl.

I ground my teeth and set my attention back to my own calculus. I didn't care if she was scared, and I didn't care how mature she looked in that form-fitting dress.

She'd already earned me a few good whacks from Hugo. It wasn't bad compared to some of the punishments he'd doled out on my father's behalf, but it still rankled that she'd caused me to be disciplined. Usually if I was beaten, it was because I intentionally got myself into trouble.

No matter what I did, I never captured my father's attention. Only Hugo's disciplinary fists. Vicente Rodríguez needed an heir, not a beloved son. His right-hand man dealt with all the things that bored him, and that included me.

My eyes roved back to Valentina's face. Her features were delicate, almost fragile. I suspected her skin was usually a glowing shade of bronze, but now, she appeared ashen. Her lower lip quivered as Mrs. Gómez lectured her on the gaps in her knowledge. Valentina's white teeth sank into her lip, making me realize how full and pouty they were. Her long, thick lashes lowered, fanning her cheeks.

This girl was young and innocent, no matter how Mariana had dressed her.

Something hot pumped through my veins. I didn't need her in my life, in my house. Taking up my space. She was just here to be my father's whore one day, when she was old enough for him to fuck her.

My fist clenched, and my pencil snapped in my hand.

Her chocolate eyes lifted in alarm, fixing on me. I glowered at her, resenting her presence. Her mouth opened slightly, her lush lips parting. A visible tremor raced through her curvy body.

The heat in my veins burned, pulsing through me and reaching areas that were embarrassing. I wasn't an inexperienced virgin, but I'd never been forced into the same space with a girl as delectable as Valentina. Suddenly, I had difficulty controlling my body.

I slammed the broken pencil down on the table and surged to my feet, grabbing up my books at the same time and strategically placing them over my growing erection.

Without a word to her or Mrs. Gómez, I stalked off to my bedroom. I'd have to deal with this problem. I'd never associated shame with sexual arousal before. Over the last year, I'd gotten the satisfaction I needed from one of the young maids who lived on father's estate.

But now, I couldn't control myself. All I wanted was to wrap Valentina's silky hair around my fist and force her to her knees. I wanted to know what those plump lips felt like caressing my cock, what those big brown eyes looked like when she was staring up at me. Would she tremble for me while she knelt at my feet?

Fuck! The visceral, fevered fantasy was almost enough to make me come undone, and I hadn't even reached my bedroom. My shaft was painfully hard, pressing against the books I held to cover my arousal. I barely made it into my room without finishing in my pants. As it was, I only had to stroke myself a few times to reach completion, finding a flicker of relief from the tension she'd incited inside me.

An unfamiliar sense of shame rolled through my body, searing my gut. Not only had I lost control like an inexperienced boy, but I'd been fantasizing about a girl who was too young for me, too innocent for my secret depravities.

Her innocence wasn't mine to take. She'd been brought here for my father to enjoy. Just because he wasn't going to fuck her until she was older didn't mean I could touch her.

Now that she was in Vicente's home, Valentina was nothing more than a possession. But she didn't belong to me.

※

Whether I liked it or not, Valentina was forced into my life. Over the next month, she became part of my daily routine, being treated almost like a daughter in Vicente's home.

Or like a lamb he was raising for the slaughter.

Children weren't cherished on this estate—I certainly wasn't—but we did have a certain standard of living. Vicente provided us with a private tutor, and we had ample space on the grounds to exercise. Ever since I was a boy, I'd spent my time running around the edges of the estate, skirting into the jungle that bordered it on the eastern side. Now, I spent a lot more time running. It was the best way to blow off steam, exhausting myself so I couldn't become consumed by lustful thoughts of the girl trapped in my home.

The worst form of exercise was when we went swimming. The first time I'd seen Valentina's curves in her demure one-piece bathing suit, I'd almost come in my shorts.

I hadn't been back to the pool since.

I resented her presence in my home.

I resented her temptation.

I resented her innocence.

And yet, I found myself watching her. Wanting her. Stalking her.

I was ashamed of my weakness, but I couldn't help myself.

Now, I stood at the threshold to the media room, where Valentina lounged on the couch by herself. My father never came in here; this was where I played my video games. Vicente had no interest in my pastimes.

But I hadn't played a game in weeks, because Valentina liked to come here in the afternoons and watch telenovelas.

Until today, I'd avoided being in this room with her. I'd found other ways to occupy my time, since she'd taken over my space.

I leaned my shoulder against the doorframe, half-hiding my body in shadow. Her dark eyes were glued to the drama unfolding in her show. Onscreen, a couple shared a passionate kiss. Valentina giggled and blushed.

The sound sent waves of heat rolling through my body, and I recognized the telltale signs of my rising desire.

Then, her laugher faded, and she touched her fingers to her lips, rubbing them lightly as she watched the couple kissing.

A low growl slipped between my teeth, a hungry sound I'd never made before.

She gasped and jolted to attention, sitting bolt upright and turning to face me. Her wide eyes met mine, and she trembled.

Another feral rumble eased up from my chest, something savage and cruel.

I'd liked the sound of her laugh, but her fear was intoxicating.

"What do you want?" she asked tremulously, sinking back into the couch cushions.

I set my jaw and lifted my chin, struggling to master the lust raging through my system.

She's too young.

She's not mine.

The second thought made my stomach twist. Valentina belonged to my father, even if he hadn't touched her yet.

"I want my room back," I said tersely, lying to cover my raging emotions. In this moment, I didn't give a fuck about my video games.

"I'm sorry," she squeaked. "I didn't know this was your room."

"Turn that shit off," I snapped, striding toward her. I was closing the distance between us. I paused when I loomed over her. She cringed into the couch, as though she could sink into it and hide from me.

I reached down and grabbed the remote from where it rested on the cushion beside her. She tried to grab it at the same time, and both our hands closed around the device. My fingers brushed hers, and an electric current jolted up my arm, sizzling deeper into my body.

Grinding my teeth, I yanked the remote away from her. Her chocolate eyes began to shine, and her lower lip trembled.

Something dropped in my chest. I'd liked her fear, but I didn't enjoy her tears. She'd been sad and quiet ever since she'd arrived on my father's estate.

"Why are you crying?" I demanded.

Her small hands suddenly curled to fists at her sides, her body tensing with anger. "Because you're mean!" she flung at me. Tears rolled down her cheeks, and a sob hitched in her throat. "You're acting like this is my fault, but I don't want to be in your space. I don't want to be here. I miss my family. I just want to go home."

She tucked her knees up to her chest, hugging them tightly. She ducked her head, hiding her face from me as her shoulders shook on a harsher sob.

I stared down at her, my stomach knotting.

Suddenly, I was sitting on the couch beside her, and

my arm wrapped around her trembling body. I'd never touched her before, and her soft warmth sank into my skin, warming my insides. This wasn't a blazing heat; it didn't further incite my lust and rage. It felt comforting, even though I was the one offering solace.

I should say something, but I couldn't seem to formulate any words. Any reassurance felt like a false platitude. Valentina wasn't going back to her family, and it wasn't within my power to grant her wish.

Sighing, I tightened my hold on her, my hand slipping from her shoulder to curve into her waist, tucking her into my side. She remained stiff against me, but I held her anyway. She felt too fucking good to release her, even if she was crying.

"It's my birthday," she mumbled into her knees, a miserable declaration.

I didn't share her misery. Instead, hope flared in my chest.

She's fifteen. Less than two years younger than me.

I jerked my head to the side, shaking the thought away. Her age didn't matter.

She's not mine.

My fingers bit into her waist, hard enough to leave a mark. She sucked in a little gasp, but she stopped shaking. She sniffled, her tears drying up.

"Sorry," she said thickly before trying to pull away from me.

I held her fast, not wanting to release her.

I didn't say anything, but I picked up the remote

again and turned up the volume, a silent indication that she could continue watching her show. It was her birthday, after all. I could at least let her enjoy her insipid drama.

She went still beside me, her attention returning to the screen. After several minutes, she zoned out, her body relaxing. As we continued watching TV, her head canted to the side, dropping to rest on my shoulder.

The warmth in my chest glowed hotter, an almost uncomfortable sensation. I'd never shared physical contact like this with anyone. I'd been with a woman before, but that had been for my sexual satisfaction. This was more intimate than burying my cock inside a hot cunt. It set my teeth on edge, but all my muscles relaxed. My grip on her waist eased, my hold firm but not bruising. She felt good tucked beside me, fitting against my body perfectly.

I spent the rest of the afternoon cuddled up on the couch with her, my furious lust finally cooling somewhat. I still wanted her, but my maddened desire was soothed.

Her breathing turned deep and even, and I realized she'd fallen asleep with her head resting on my shoulder. Finally giving into the temptation that had tormented me for weeks, I touched her hair, trailing my fingers through the dark, silky locks. She was just as soft as I'd imagined in my fevered fantasies.

She sighed in her sleep and snuggled closer to me. My hand stilled on her head, but when she didn't wake,

I resumed stroking her, exploring. She smelled good. Not artificially sweet like Mariana, but a natural, feminine scent that called to my more primal instincts.

I squeezed my eyes shut, cursing my unruly body as my cock began to stiffen. I drew in several deep breaths, but that only made her scent suffuse my senses.

I stood abruptly, putting distance between us. She let out a little surprised squeak as she slid down onto the couch, no longer supported by my arm around her.

I had a heartbeat to register her wide, shocked stare before I tore myself away and stalked out of the room. Even in her sleep, Valentina tempted me to the edge of my control.

The air was hot and heavy, my sweaty t-shirt sticking to my skin. I slowed to a jog as I neared the house, decreasing my speed from sprinting. My lungs burned from exertion; I'd been running as though I could exhaust my desire for Valentina from my system. I couldn't stop thinking about how soft she'd been against me yesterday, how good she'd smelled as she sighed and snuggled closer.

Frustrated and overheated, I stripped off my wet shirt and tossed it aside, pausing to stretch out my overworked muscles.

After a few minutes, the back of my neck prickled with awareness. Someone was watching me.

I jerked upright, searching for the threat.

I froze, my body going rigid in response to her wide-eyed stare. Valentina stood only a few yards away on the front porch, her lips parted as she looked at me. Her dark gaze wasn't fixed on mine. Her eyes roved over my body, studying me with open fascination. My arms flexed, my abs rippling as tension rolled through my body. Her tongue darted out to wet her pouty lips.

I remembered the way she'd rubbed her lips while she'd watched the couple kiss on TV. Did she know what it felt like to be kissed? Had anyone ever tasted her lush mouth?

Judging by her shocked study of my body, I doubted it. Her innocence made something dark coil in my chest, and my gut tightened with desire.

I studied her body, in return. She wore a tight white t-shirt that strained over her breasts, and her tanned legs were on display beneath the far-too-short exercise shorts she wore. If she turned around, I'd be able to see her thighs all the way up to the lower curve of her ass.

I should have been enraged that someone had bought these skimpy clothes to display her body, but all I could focus on was the hunger that made my mouth water.

"What are you doing out here?" I asked, my voice deeper and more gravelly than I'd ever heard it.

She swallowed and licked her lips again, her eyes straying to my heaving chest. "I... I thought I'd go for a run."

"With me?" Surprise flickered through my mind. Yes, she'd let me hold her when she was vulnerable yesterday, but she also feared me. She thought I was mean.

And I supposed I was. I could be cruel, and my fantasies about her certainly bordered on sadistic.

"Um, yeah," she said breathily. "I didn't feel like swimming today."

If the girl thought we were friends after the comfort I'd offered her yesterday, she was mistaken. I didn't want to be her friend. I didn't want her in my home, tempting and tormenting me.

She'd been right to fear me. I'd have to ensure that she didn't mistake my brief show of compassion for kindness.

A wicked smile tugged at one corner of my lips. She took a wary step back.

I bit back a groan. Her trepidation was intoxicating. I liked when she was afraid of me. It made me feel powerful in a way I'd never known before. I was accustomed to being inconsequential, barely worth noticing. When I was with Valentina, I commanded her full attention.

"Come here, *conejita*." The command dropped from my lips on a low purr, something soft and dangerous. I wanted my frightened little bunny to come to me, to place herself at my mercy.

My thought processes were becoming muddled. I'd intended to drive her away by reminding her to be afraid of me, but now, I craved her nearness. But I still wanted her fear.

She closed the distance between us, her steps hesitant. She was afraid, but she obeyed.

A heady sensation rushed through me, making me feel warm and a little dizzy, like I had the night I'd snuck into Vicente's liquor cabinet.

When she was only a few feet away from me, I took the final step between us, my body drawn to hers as though by a magnet. I asserted myself in her personal space, towering over her petite frame. A shudder raced through her body, and her pulse jumped at her throat.

"Run," I ordered softly.

"What?" Her lashes fluttered, her question little more than a whisper.

"Run, *conejita*. I'll give you thirty seconds."

Her dark brows drew together. "Thirty seconds? What happens after that?"

"I catch you."

Suddenly, her lips tilted in a saucy grin. The sight of her joy knocked the air from my chest. She was practically incandescent when she smiled, the mischievous glint in her eye only serving to sharpen my predatory hunger for her.

"You can try," she taunted, turning from me and racing off.

She was fast. Faster than I would have thought. Over the last month, I'd only seen a meek, soft-spoken girl practically tiptoeing through my house.

Now, Valentina bounded across the grass, heading straight for the jungle. A low growl tore from my chest, and my muscles practically vibrated with the need to chase after her.

I took a deep breath and started counting down the seconds. She'd almost reached the tree line when I launched after her. Entering the jungle would slow her down. It wasn't too dense this close to the estate, but she'd still have to contend with the natural barriers created by the vegetation.

Maybe she thought she had a better chance of evading me under the cover of the trees.

She was mistaken.

My senses heightened like I'd never known. I could hear her tearing through the jungle ahead of me, and I was hyperaware of the coolness of the air rushing over my burning flesh as I sprinted across the yard.

Valentina was my prey, and she didn't have a hope of escaping capture.

A snarl rumbled up my throat, and her melodic, breathless laugh wove through the trees, floating back to me and betraying her location.

She'd slowed, perhaps pausing to catch her breath. I couldn't hear her feet pounding against the earth anymore. All I had to go on was the direction of her laugh. After a few seconds of pursuit, I heard her heavy breathing. I slowed to a prowl, moving almost silently through the familiar wilderness.

A feral sound slipped between my teeth as I darted

around the tree that sheltered her. She shrieked in surprise when I grabbed her, and she tried to twist away from me.

My hands sank into her waist, and I tackled her to the ground, turning my body so I bore the brunt of the impact with the damp earth. She gasped at the shock of the fall, and I took advantage of her disorientated state.

I rolled atop her, settling my weight over her slight body. She lifted her hands, blindly shoving at my chest. A shaky laugh burst from her lips as adrenaline coursed through her system, making her shake beneath me.

I grabbed her wrists, yanking her arms above her head and pinning them to the dirt. Her laughter strangled in her throat, turning into something like a whimper. The sound made my lust rush through my veins, and my cock stiffened against her belly. Her eyes flew wide, and she squirmed beneath me. The writhing movement stimulated my dick, and I growled down at her, acting like the animal I was. In that moment, I fully unleashed my predatory instincts, thoroughly subjugating my prey.

She shivered and softened, going still beneath me. Her chest rose and fell on rapid, panting breaths, and her pupils dilated. Her pulse thrummed at her throat. My gaze fixed on the little pulsing line at her vulnerable neck.

Without thinking, I dipped my head forward. My tongue snaked out to trace the line of her artery. Her salty flavor suffused my system, obliterating rational thought. I retreated to a purely primal headspace, and my teeth sank into her shoulder, pinning her beneath me. She whimpered again, twisting against me. I increased the intensity of my bite, holding her firmly until she shuddered and stilled.

Satisfied with her surrender, I released her and traced the little indentations my teeth had left in her skin, flicking my tongue over her abused flesh. A harsh sound caught in her throat, as though she was swallowing a sharp cry. Her back arched, her breasts pressing against my bare chest. She wasn't writhing in an effort to escape me anymore. She rubbed herself against me, her hips rotating up into my thigh.

I pulled back from her neck, so I could stare down into her eyes. She gazed up at me, almost as though she were in a trance. I saw confusion flicker across her features. My innocent Valentina didn't understand what was happening to her, what I was awakening within her body.

I crushed my lips to hers, knowing I was the first to claim her mouth. She stiffened beneath me for a moment, but I sank my teeth into her lower lip in rebuke. She shivered and gasped, and my tongue surged into her open mouth. For a few heartbeats, she didn't respond, not knowing how to accept my kiss. I stroked into her mouth, silently instructing her how to surrender to me. Tentatively, she moved her tongue against mine, and I groaned at the decadent sensation of her innocent exploration.

She jerked in my grip, her hands instinctively seeking to touch me. I couldn't allow that. If she did, I would come apart, and I wouldn't ruin this perfect sense of complete power by losing control of my body.

I lowered my hands slightly, digging my fingers into her forearms as I shoved her down into the soft earth. She drew in a shuddering breath, and I kissed her with more force, taking everything I wanted from her. Her soft whimpers and little panting sounds when I allowed her to breathe drove me to the brink of madness, but her total submission gave me the sense of control I needed to deny my base urges. I might be pressing her body into the dirt, but I wouldn't soil my innocent Valentina.

She's not mine.

The cruel thought ripped through my mind, shattering the perfection of the encounter. I'd never be able to have the girl who felt so perfect, pinned beneath me and trembling with equal parts fear and desire.

I pushed up off her with a curse, tearing my lips from hers.

She stared up at me, her eyes glassy and dazed, her lips swollen and glistening from my brutal kiss.

My fingers curled to fists at my sides, and I gnashed my teeth like the animal I was before I turned sharply and sprinted away. I had to put distance between us, before I did something I couldn't take back.

CHAPTER 4
VALENTINA

My lips still tingled from Adrián's fierce kiss. After he'd left me alone and confused in the jungle, my limbs had felt oddly heavy and my cheeks were hot. Even though my mind reeled from the strange events and his sudden abandonment, my body still burned.

I'd taken a shower, and my skin had felt almost unbearably sensitive beneath the warm spray. My nipples were hard, and my sex pulsed strangely. I didn't understand what was happening to me, but I knew it felt good. Strange and a little scary, but *so good.*

I got into bed, my skin feeling tight. A place low in my belly ached. I pulled the covers over my head and squeezed my eyes shut, as though that would help blot out the strange sensations.

Suddenly, the mattress dipped.

I yelped and threw the covers off, my heart hammering against my ribcage.

Adrian's pale green eyes burned down into me, his granite jaw tight and his defined cheekbones sharper than ever. He sat on the edge of my bed, as though he had every right to be in my private space.

I shrank away, fear stirring at the back of my mind as my blood pumped hotter through my veins. The ache between my legs intensified, pulsing in time with my heartbeat.

Before I could demand to know what he was doing in my room, he reached out and rubbed his thumb across my lower lip. Sparks danced over my skin, spreading through my flesh and finding their way deeper inside me. My brain buzzed, and electricity crackled through my body.

"You left me," I said without thinking, my voice strangely breathy and a little petulant.

"I did." He didn't stop touching me. His fingers moved from my lips to trail over my cheeks, to trace the line of my jaw. He barely brushed my skin, but when he touched my thrumming pulse at my neck, I arched toward him on a gasp. "I'm here now," he rumbled.

"Why?" I managed to ask, even though my mind reeled and my body was doing strange, distracting things. There was something wet between my thighs, and my nipples peaked against my silky nightgown.

"Because I can't stay away," he rasped.

His touch left my throat, and he pressed lightly on

the bruises he'd left on my forearms. His eyes darkened, and his lips curved with malicious pleasure as I shuddered. He inflicted a slight flare of pain on the tender areas, but the wetness between my legs became slicker, and a small spot at the top of my sex pulsed.

"What are you doing to me?" I asked on a strangled whisper.

"I know you must be aching," he said instead of answering my question.

"What do you mean?"

"Your pussy hurts, doesn't it?"

"My what?"

His lips pressed together on a low growl, his features drawing tight with something sharp I didn't understand.

"The place between your legs," he ground out. "Does it ache? Are you wet for me?"

"I don't know..." I was very aware of the dampness on my sex. "What's happening?"

He caressed my cheek, rubbing my lips again. My lashes fluttered as heat rolled through my body. "My innocent *conejita*," he said roughly. "I'm going to help you. Do you know how to make yourself feel good?"

I swallowed, my tongue feeling too thick in my mouth. I wanted him to kiss me again. I wanted him to hold me down and leave more marks on my skin.

"I... I don't know what you mean."

"When I leave, I want you to rub the little bud at the top of your pussy. I want you to rub it and think about me." His eyes turned feverish, his words gravelly.

"Why do you have to leave?" My voice came out low and husky. I didn't want him to go.

His jaw ticked. "Because I can't watch you come, or I'll do something I shouldn't."

He leaned over me, and I tilted my head back, welcoming him to claim my lips again. Instead, he pressed a tender kiss against my forehead. He nuzzled my hair, inhaling deeply.

"Be a good girl and do what I told you," he murmured in my ear, his hot breath teasing across my neck. A high whine eased up my throat, and he pressed another kiss to my heated skin, on my neck this time. I turned my face, inviting him to bite me again.

He jerked away and got to his feet. He stared down at me, the lines of his powerful body tense. His pale eyes seared into my soul. "I'll be next door in my room, thinking about you," he promised.

I didn't fully understand what he meant, but pleasure rushed through me at the prospect of him thinking of me. Would he touch himself, too? Would he caress the hard bulge I'd felt against my belly when he held me down in the jungle? I didn't know how men and women were together other than kissing, but I instinctively knew the hard ridge that had pressed into me meant something dark and tempting.

He turned from me and walked stiffly out of my room, closing the door softly behind him. Compelled by my body's needs and his command, I reached beneath the sheets and touched my sex. I found the hard bud he'd mentioned, rubbing it tentatively. Heat flashed through my body, and a low moan left my chest. I'd never felt anything like this. It felt forbidden and so good. I couldn't stop myself from seeking more stimulation.

I thought about how Adrián had held me down in the jungle, the scorching heat of his body bearing down on mine, the biting pain of his teeth and his cruel fingers around my arms.

Pleasure rushed through me, and I bit my lip to hold in a soft cry.

I lay back, my muscles loose and my breaths coming fast and hard. I melted into the mattress, languor rolling over me. In a matter of minutes, I fell into deep, peaceful sleep.

❧

SOMETHING HOT AND WET COATED MY INNER THIGHS, and the sheets were damp beneath me. I stirred, the morning light rousing me as well as the uncomfortable tightness in my belly. This wasn't the darkly delicious tension that had gripped me when I'd touched myself and thought of Adrián. This hurt, my muscles cramping and twisting.

I looked beneath the sheets, and a high shriek ripped up my throat. I was bleeding. Dark crimson soaked the sheets beneath me. It was coated on my legs. Was this the wetness I'd felt last night when

Adrián had stared down at me and ordered me to rub myself?

I hadn't been hurting at the time, but I hadn't looked down to check what was happening to my body. I'd just done as he commanded, losing myself in pleasure.

I cried out again at a sharp twist in my belly.

My bedroom door slammed against the wall with the force of Adrián's entry. His shirtless form filled the threshold, his pale eyes wide and watchful, as though searching for a threat.

Panic slammed into my chest, and I drew the covers up to my chin, hiding the mess. Shame burned through my cheeks.

"Get out!" I shouted.

"Are you okay?" he asked, his voice heavy with concern and his brows drawn in confusion.

"Leave me alone," I railed at him. "Go away!"

"What the hell is going on?" Mariana appeared behind Adrián. For once, her face wasn't painted with makeup, and I could see fine lines around her eyes.

She took one look at my panicked expression, and her lips pursed. "Go back to bed, Adrián," she said, more calmly. "This is women's business, I think."

He paled. "Oh."

He moved out of Mariana's way, slipping back into the shadowed hallway. I heard his bedroom door close, the sharp snap reverberating through my chest. I was frightened, and suddenly, I didn't want him to leave me alone with Mariana.

She approached me, her dark eyes soft with understanding. "You started your period?" she asked, her tone uncharacteristically kind.

"I'm bleeding," I whimpered, not knowing what she was talking about.

She nodded. "You're a woman now," she told me.

My stomach twisted, nausea rising.

Is she a woman yet? Vicente's ominous question rang through my mind.

"I'm not," I choked. "I'm just a girl."

Mariana shook her head. "You're still young, but you're not a little girl anymore."

Tears rolled down my cheeks, my emotions swinging.

She shushed me. "It's okay. This is a natural part of being a woman. You're not hurt."

"My stomach aches," I sniffled. "And I don't want to be a woman."

"You have to grow up at some point." She sighed. "But I'll make sure Vicente stays away. You're not old enough yet."

"Old enough for what?" I asked, my voice small.

Her full lips pressed together. "I'll explain what happens between men and women to you later. For now, let's get this mess cleaned up. Go take a shower, and I'll call a maid to change the sheets. I'll give you some tampons, too."

"Tampons?" I didn't know the word.

"They help manage the bleeding," she said. "I guess I need to explain more to you than I thought. Didn't your mother tell you about this?"

A sob wracked my chest. "I don't have a mother. *Abuela* didn't tell me about...about this." I didn't have the vocabulary to express what was happening to my body. All I knew was that I'd started bleeding after I'd touched myself. After Adrián had kissed me.

You're a woman now.

My body was changing, and it was Adrián's fault.

THAT NIGHT, MY STOMACH STILL CRAMPED, BUT Mariana had given me some medicine to manage the discomfort. The tampon had hurt when I'd first put it in, so she'd given me pads instead. The thick lining in my underwear was uncomfortable between my legs, a cruel reminder of my newfound maturity.

I hadn't gone to our tutoring session today. I'd barely left my bed. Despair weighed heavy in my chest. Mariana had explained sex to me this morning, and the very concept made nausea rise in my throat. Vicente wanted to do that to me. He wanted to put his penis inside me and take my virginity.

My eyes burned, but I didn't have any more tears to cry; they'd dried up hours ago. Mariana had promised that she would delay Vicente for a few years. But my fate was sealed. I was trapped in his home, waiting for the day he'd claim me.

For the hundredth time that day, my mind flitted to the memory of Adrián holding me down in the jungle. I understood what the thick ridge against my belly had been now. Mariana had explained male arousal to me. My mind reeled with the disgusting information she'd burdened me with.

Only, it didn't seem as disgusting when I thought of Adrián. Even though I was horrified by the concept of sex, my body still heated at the thought of his powerful arms pinning me down, the memory of his demanding lips subjugating my mouth.

My bedroom door creaked open.

"Please leave me alone," I begged, my voice small. I kept my eyes closed. I didn't want to hear anything else Mariana had to say. I couldn't take anymore.

"I know you're bleeding, but I don't care about that."

I let out a soft cry of alarm, and I jolted upright, clutching the sheets to my chest. Hugo entered my room, closing the door behind him.

"What are you doing here?" I squeaked.

"Mariana told Vicente and me. You're a woman today. He wants to wait, but he's a fool." Hugo prowled toward me. Panic fluttered in my chest, urging me to flee.

But there was nowhere for me to go. His doughy

body blocked my only exit, and if I got out of bed, he'd see me wearing nothing but my nightgown.

"This will be our little secret," he told me, his thin lips curved in a lascivious smile. A bulge appeared in his slacks, and I now recognized the sign of male desire. "I'll make sure you take up horseback riding. Vicente will never know why your hymen is broken."

I pulled the covers up higher, as though they could serve as a shield between us. "Leave me alone." I tried to sound strong and defiant, but it came out as a horrified whisper.

He reached my bed. Forgetting my modesty, I tried to roll away, struggling to get to my feet and evade him somehow.

His thick fingers tangled in my hair, jerking me back and yanking me down. His weight settled over me, crushing the air from my chest. I drew in a desperate breath and let it out on a terrified scream. His meaty hand clamped over my mouth. I twisted, shoving at his chest. He caught my flailing arms, pinning them above my head with his free hand. I was trapped, helpless. When Adrián had held me so ruthlessly in the jungle, my body had softened for him. Now, I tensed and jerked, fear thrumming through me. Horror suffused my system when Hugo didn't budge.

He was going to have sex with me. He was going to take my virginity, and there was nothing I could do to stop him.

My panicked shriek was muffled by his hand on my

mouth, and his fingers bit into my cheeks as he held me down with brutal strength.

A feral roar filled the room, reverberating through my body. Hugo was torn from me, and I sucked in a desperate breath as his weight left my chest.

Adrián tackled him to the floor, their bodies hitting the hardwoods with a dull thud. Adrián brought his fist down on Hugo's jaw, and blood sprayed from his lips as his head snapped to the side.

But Hugo was bigger than Adrián. The bulky man wrestled the boy, managing to pin him. Suddenly, he was the one delivering the beating, and I screamed as his fists slammed into Adrián's face.

"Stop!" I shrieked. "Please, stop!"

Hugo's attention jerked to me for a moment, his beady eyes narrowing on me. Adrián took advantage of his distraction, gaining the upper hand again. He landed another punch across Hugo's jaw, and the older man reeled back. Adrián shoved him down, his fingers curling into Hugo's shirt as he slammed him against the floor.

"She's not yours!" he snarled into Hugo's face, blood dripping from his lips.

Hugo abruptly held up his hands in a show of surrender. "Fine," he hissed. "She belongs to Vicente. Don't even think about tattling on me to your father, boy," he added, his voice soft with menace.

"You don't come near her again," Adrián bit out. "You don't touch her."

Hugo shoved him away, and Adrián allowed the doughy man to get to his feet. He shot a contemptuous sneer my way, then turned sharply and stalked out of my room.

Adrián's fists clenched at his sides, his body practically vibrating with lingering violence. Suddenly, he rounded on me, his green eyes blazing. I shrank back, but he advanced on me anyway. His hands closed around my upper arms, yanking me against his hard chest.

"No one touches you," he growled at me.

"Adrián," I whimpered his name. "You're scaring me."

His grip on my arms eased, and he pulled me into a tight embrace. I heard him inhale deeply, and he nuzzled my hair. He dropped a tender kiss on my shoulder. I felt the warmth of his blood on my skin. My own blood heated, even as I trembled in his arms.

"Don't be scared, *conejita*," he murmured. "I won't let him touch you. No one touches you," he said again, his voice dropping deeper as his arms firmed around me. "You're mine."

From that moment on, I belonged to Adrián.

CHAPTER 5
ADRIÁN

One Year Later

"Happy Birthday, *conejita*." I cuddled Valentina closer, and she snuggled into my bare chest with a happy sigh. For a year, I'd snuck into her room and slept with her almost every night. We spent our days together, too: studying, watching her telenovelas, playing chess. And playing rougher, darker games when I chased her through the jungle. We were inseparable, and I didn't think I'd know how to breathe if I weren't sharing the same air as Valentina.

I'd never allowed myself to do more than kiss her, even though it caused me physical pain to deny myself. The longer I possessed her, the more obsessed I became with preserving her innocence. I'd keep her safe from everyone, even myself. I still held her with harsh passion, some of my sadism bleeding out on occasion. I left marks on her skin with my hands and my teeth, but I didn't allow myself more. I'd never even touched her bare body. I'd never seen her naked.

The temptation to fuck her would overwhelm me if I did.

I'd definitely never allowed her to touch my cock, no matter how keenly I craved her small hands caressing my length.

I couldn't despoil my innocent Valentina. She was far too pure and sweet to endure all the dark, perverted things I wanted to do to her.

That didn't stop the cruel fantasies of binding her in place for my pleasure and making her scream my name as I marked her flesh in different ways. Sometimes, when we rode horses together, I thought about taking the whip in my hand and lashing her with it. I didn't understand why I wanted to hurt her and cherish her at the same time, but my obsession drove me to the edge of sanity.

Now, I was calmer, finding some measure of peace as she trailed her soft fingers over my skin, tracing the contours of my muscles. I ran my hand through her hair, addicted to the way the silken strands fell through my fingers. She hummed and leaned into my touch, welcoming more.

"I love you."

Her fervent declaration knifed through my chest, piercing my heart and twisting. Something hot and feral raced through my veins, and I settled my weight over her, pinning her down.

"What did you say?" I growled.

She blinked up at me, her chocolate eyes wide and earnest. "I love you," she repeated.

She'd never said the words before.

My fingers bit into her wrists where I held them above her head. "Don't say that," I ground out.

"Why? I love you, Adrián."

"Stop saying that!" I barked, even as the knife in my chest burned white-hot.

No one had ever told me they loved me. My mother had abandoned me when I was a baby, leaving me behind when she ran away from my father's cruelty. And Vicente had certainly never expressed affection for me.

"But I do," she insisted, not flinching away from my brutality. "I'm yours, Adrián. I'm yours, and I love you."

A curse dropped from my lips, and heat pricked at the corners of my eyes.

Her brow wrinkled. "Why are you upset? Don't you... Don't you love me?"

"Of course I love you!" I shouted at her. "Of course I do," I rasped, my voice dropping to something more ragged.

"Then why are you crying?"

I realized my cheeks were wet. "Because I have to let you go." I spoke the truth I'd never wanted to acknowledge. For a year, I'd known it deep in my soul. But I was selfish and desperate for her, so I'd ignored it.

"What are you talking about?" she asked, her eyes wide with alarm. "I'm not going anywhere. I belong with you."

"Because you're not mine," I seethed, my fingers tightening around her wrists. Wet heat dripped down from my face to splash on her cheek. "You belong to Vicente. I won't let him have you," I hissed. "You're leaving this estate. I'm going to get you out."

"You're wrong," she said fiercely. "I am yours. And you're mine."

"You have to leave." The words caught in my throat as misery settled heavy in my gut. I didn't know how to live without her anymore. I didn't know if my heart could beat without hers.

"Then you're coming with me," she declared. I might be holding her down, but she didn't cower and submit. She was still full of fire, determination. "I love you, Adrián. If I'm leaving, we're going together."

"I can't," I said tightly. "I'm Vicente's heir. He won't let me go. If I come with you, he'll hunt us down."

"Then let him try. I know you'll keep me safe. I trust you with my life, Adrián. I can't live without you." Her fervent declaration echoed my own feelings.

"I can't live without you, either." The admission was drawn from deep in my soul. "I love you, Valentina." I sealed my promise with a brutal kiss. I'd find a way to get her out. I wouldn't let anyone have her, especially not my father.

Valentina was mine.

"Valentina, you're late for breakfast." Mariana's peeved voice roused me, along with the sound of the bedroom door creaking open. "What the hell is going on here?" Her sharp exclamation jolted me awake.

Fuck! I rolled away from Valentina, stumbling to my feet. Sleep still fogged my mind, and my morning wood strained against my boxers. I'd never stayed with her this late into the morning, and now, we'd been discovered together.

I blinked hard and focused on Mariana. Her jaw gaped, her eyes dropping to my erection before narrowing.

"Wait until your father hears about this," she hissed.

Before I could formulate a coherent thought, she raced out of the bedroom.

I cursed aloud, my gaze finding Valentina. Her dark eyes were wide with panic.

"Go," she said, desperate. "Get out of here."

"She'll tell Vicente," I said, my own voice heavy with horror. I didn't know what my father would do, but it wouldn't be anything good. "I can't leave you."

"You have to," she said urgently, her attention dropping to my dick. I was still hard for her. "Go to your room. Get dressed. Hurry."

I ran a hand through my hair, indecision ripping at my insides. I didn't want to leave her unprotected, but I couldn't stay here, nearly naked. Even if I managed to get the last of my arousal under control, the evidence of my state of undress was damning.

"I'll get us out of this," I promised. "I'll keep you safe. I love you." The words were new, but I didn't want to stop saying them, now that we'd admitted our feelings.

"I love you, too," she swore, even as she made a little shooing motion. "Go!"

I bolted out of her room, darting into my own bedroom to tug on my clothes. I'd barely managed to get into my jeans before my door crashed open.

"What the fuck have you done?" Vicente raged.

But it wasn't my father who came barreling at me. Hugo's weight slammed into me, taking me to the floor. His fist smashed into my jaw, and stars burst across my vision. He'd hit me plenty of times, but I understood in that moment that he'd always held back the full force of his brutality. My world spun, my stomach lurching as nausea spiked.

I shook my head hard to clear it, but Hugo's weight kept me pinned.

"I love her," I snarled, struggling to breathe when Hugo was crushing my chest.

His fist smashed into my face again. I tasted blood in my mouth, and the world flickered around me. Meaty hands jerked me upright before slamming me back against the wall. Dizziness washed over me, my nausea coming in waves.

I blinked hard, and my father's face came into focus.

He loomed beside Hugo, who held me fast. I tried to shove him away, and his hands closed around my throat, squeezing hard enough to cut off my air supply. I grabbed at his arms, struggling to break his iron hold. But I was disoriented by his blows to my head, and my fingers started to go numb as I clawed at him.

"You are no longer welcome in this house," Vicente seethed. "You're going to America. You're a man now. It's time you started acting like it."

I jerked my head to the side, my refusal catching in my trapped throat.

"You're going to run my business in California," he continued. "If you ever try to come back to Colombia, I'll kill her. Do you hear me? Valentina dies if you step foot on this estate."

Black spots danced across my vision, blotting out his enraged face. My arms stopped working, dropping to my sides as my limbs turned to lead.

Fear for Valentina followed me down into darkness, but there was nothing I could do to resist oblivion.

CHAPTER 6

VALENTINA

"Where's Adrián?" I demanded as soon as Vicente stormed into my bedroom. Mariana had locked me in and left me alone. It felt like hours has passed since I'd heard the sounds of a physical struggle coming from Adrián's bedroom. The silence that followed had stretched on and on, driving me to the edge of madness. I couldn't hear him moving around in his bedroom next door. I couldn't see him. I couldn't touch him, feeling his heartbeat beneath my hand to know he was with me and I was safe.

"He's gone," Vicente replied coldly. He cocked his head at me, stroking his beard as his black eyes roved over my body. I realized I was still wearing my silky nightgown, and it barely concealed my nakedness.

I wrapped my arms around my chest in a vain attempt to hide from his assessing gaze.

His lips curved in a contemptuous sneer. "I don't want something my son has touched," he announced.

Even though he talked about me as though I was an object rather than a person, relief slammed through my system. Vicente didn't want me anymore. I was free to be with Adrián.

"Gone where?" I demanded. Wherever Adrián had been sent, I would follow.

"To America," Vicente told me, his lips peeled back with rage.

I lifted my chin. "Then I'm going, too."

"You're not going anywhere," Vicente seethed.

"Why?" I demanded, desperate to get packed and go to Adrián. "I'm not yours."

He studied me in silence for a few long seconds. "You love him," he said coldly.

"I do," I replied fiercely. "You can't keep us apart."

His black eyes glinted with malice. "I can and I will. Hugo!" he barked out for his friend.

I took an involuntary step back when Hugo's bulky body appeared behind Vicente's.

"She's yours now, Hugo," Vicente announced, never taking his eyes off me.

Ice crystalized in my veins, and I took another step back. "No."

Hugo's thin lips split in a leer, and he advanced on me. I tried to dodge away, but his big hands wrapped around my arms, yanking me against his rounded belly. I shrieked and twisted against his grip. I felt his hard arousal pressing into my belly.

"Wait for your wedding night," Vicente drawled. "If you want her to give you an heir, make it official."

"No," this time, the refusal left me on a horrified moan. "I won't marry you. I won't. I love Adrián."

"You love me from now on," Hugo hissed. His hot tongue licked at the tear that trailed down my cheek.

I gagged against the bile that rose in the back of my throat.

"Let me go," I demanded, desperate. "I want Adrián."

"You're not a little girl anymore," Vicente told me, his tone heavy with vindictive satisfaction. "What you want doesn't matter. You'll obey your husband from now on."

"He's not my husband," I shouted. I writhed in Hugo's grip. His lascivious grin filled my vision, the reek of his sickly-sweet cologne invading my senses. His cock jerked against me.

"Adrián!" I screamed for him, a foolish, childish part of me believing he'd come racing into the bedroom to save me.

He had to come save me. He had to.

But that was a stupid little girl's fantasy. I was a woman now, and Hugo made sure to teach me what that meant.

The End

What happens when Valentina and Adrián are reunited? Find out in Stealing Beauty...

Adrián seems to hate me as much as I loathe him, but that doesn't stop him from abducting me. He rescues me from one gilded cage to place me in another--one where he holds the key.

I've been trapped with my abusers for a decade, abandoned by the boy I thought would be my savior. Now that Adrián has finally come back for me, the boy I loved is gone. A hard, ruthless man has taken his place: a sadistic drug lord who wants to make me his.

The men who have tormented me for ten years want me back, and we're on the run to Adrián's territory. Despite my efforts to escape him, he drags me from Colombia to California, punishing me in the most deviant ways when I try to resist.

Even if we make it out alive, I'll never be free.

I'm far too broken and betrayed to ever love Adrián again, but he'll stop at nothing to possess me, body and soul.

Turn the page for an extended excerpt...

STEALING BEAUTY
EXCERPT

Pale green eyes sliced into my chest, their cutting gaze keener than I remembered. They practically glowed as he glowered at me from across the church: a panther deciding whether his prey was worth bothering with the hunt. His full lips curled in a sneer, those beautiful, terrifying eyes scanning my body.

Whatever he saw in me, he decided I wasn't worth his time. He blinked and looked away, his attention turning back to the stunning blonde draped on his arm.

I sucked in a gasp, remembering how to breathe. My fingers trembled at my sides as a hit of adrenaline surged through my system.

I'd known Adrián would be here. I'd told myself I was ready to face him. I'd told myself that I'd be able to mask my ire and put on the pretty, pleasant smile that was expected of me.

But I hadn't been prepared for the hatred in his

burning stare. Ten long years had passed since I'd last looked into those hypnotic green eyes. Once, they'd shined with devotion when he looked at me.

Now, it seemed he loathed me as much as I despised him.

I collected my wits, clenching my fists at my sides to still my shaking fingers. My perfectly manicured nails bit into my palms, but I welcomed the little flare of pain. It helped ground me. Pain reminded me of my role, my duties.

I'd receive a lot more of it if I didn't play my part perfectly: devoted wife to Hugo Sánchez, the second most powerful man in Bogotá.

The most powerful man, Vicente Rodríguez, was the reason I was here, participating in this farce.

A visible shiver raced through the young woman—barely more than a girl—who stood at the altar. Camila Gómez had the misfortune of catching Vicente's eye a year ago. The eighteen-year-old had gotten pregnant, giving him a son. He'd decided to force her into this marriage to ensure the boy's legitimacy. A secondary heir to his cocaine empire, in case something were to happen to Adrián.

Adrián Rodríguez. I could hardly believe the boy I'd loved all those years ago had turned into the hard, frightening man who'd taken his place in the church pew behind me. I couldn't see him, but I could feel his cruel glare on my back. It made my skin pebble with a prey's awareness, my body instinctively sensing the threat.

For the last decade, he'd been in America, consolidating the power of his father's cartel in California. I'd never expected to see him again, but Vicente's wedding to poor Camila had brought the prodigal son home to Colombia.

The girl's petite frame appeared smaller than ever as she shrank in Vicente's shadow. He'd waited long enough for her slender body to return to its youthful perfection after she'd given birth—no doubt, she was kept on a careful regimen to ensure her beauty for this day.

I was far too familiar with the practice: the restricted diet and proscribed exercise to keep my natural curves just the right size to please my husband. Mercifully, Hugo stood at Vicente's side rather than mine. As Vicente's lapdog, Hugo was a natural choice to play the part of best man at this sham wedding.

My husband's beady black eyes fixed on me, and his thin lips curved into a malicious smile. An involuntary shudder wracked my body. He'd looked at me with the exact same expression ten years ago, when I'd been the one in the pretty white dress, forced to the altar against my will. I was only sixteen at the time, but Hugo hadn't minded being wedded to a child. He'd waited too long for his turn with me to care.

And as my guardian, Vicente had given me away to

his best friend, gifting me to him in exchange for his years of loyalty.

I could hardly bear to look at either of the disgusting, lecherous men. Somehow, I lifted my chin and straightened my spine. I couldn't allow anyone in the church to sense that my fear-drenched memories of my wedding night were playing through my mind.

Hugo delighted in my fear, but he also expected me to maintain the façade of perfect, loving wife when we were in public. He might be short and stocky, but his rounded belly didn't diminish his strength. His thinning black hair and ruddy cheeks were showing the signs of his age, but the years hadn't caused him to grow frail. He was as brutal as he'd been on the day I'd met him, when I was fourteen years old.

I plastered on a beatific smile, meeting my husband's gaze. To any casual observer, I'd appear to be staring at him with love and devotion, remembering the false joy of our own wedding day.

Camila's palpable terror made the dark memories I kept locked at the back of my mind push to the forefront. I shoved them away before I gagged. A metallic tang coated my tongue, and I realized I'd bitten the inside of my cheek.

The ceremony passed by in a blur. I drew in deep breaths to suppress my rising nausea. When the priest pronounced Vicente and Camila husband and wife, I managed a wide smile. My eyes watered with empathy for the girl, but I'd be able to pass it off as tears of joy.

I followed the stream of guests as we exited the white and gold opulence of the basilica, stepping out into the heavy dusk heat. Hugo waited by the black limo outside the church, gesturing that I should get in the car. Vicente and Camila were already in their vintage Rolls-Royce, which would take them to the reception space: an imposing, historic *castillo* located outside Bogotá.

I smiled at my husband and took his hand, allowing him to help me slide into the back seat. He settled in beside me, pressing his doughy body close to mine. The sickening scent of his amber cologne mingling with his sweat washed over me. I'd become accustomed to it over the years, but today, the overpowering reek made me want to retch.

Seconds later, my nausea intensified. My gut lurched as Adrián got into the limo, his stunning blonde date sliding into place at his side. Her dark eyebrows didn't match her platinum locks, but the obvious dye job didn't diminish her beauty.

I couldn't focus on her, though. My eyes locked on Adrián's burning green stare.

My breath caught, and my pretty smile melted.

Hugo's meaty hand rested on my thigh, high enough to be indecent in front of strangers.

But Adrián wasn't a stranger. He was a ghost from my past. A horrifying apparition that appeared all too corporeal. His massive body filled the space, his bulk obvious even beneath his sharply-tailored black suit.

I could feel Hugo's hot breath on my face before he pressed a wet, stomach-turning kiss against my cheek. "Are you all right, *cariña?*"

Adrián's nostrils flared, his full lips thinning. His square jaw hardened to granite, and his high cheekbones appeared sharper than ever.

For a moment, the world spun around me, the sickly-sweet stench of my husband powerful enough to make me lightheaded.

Hugo's fingers dug into my thigh, a clear warning to behave myself.

The flare of pain helped me focus. I tore my eyes from Adrián's, staring out the window instead.

"I'm fine," I managed.

I couldn't look at my husband. I could barely draw breath when he was so close, and Adrián's hatred pressing against me like a tangible force didn't help me breathe easier.

I tried to focus on the glittering lights as the city lit up around us, the historic sites of *La Candelaria* district beginning to glow against the falling darkness. The limo's tires rumbled over cobblestones. I kept my attention on the soft, purring sound to soothe my raw nerves.

Eventually, the pavement evened out, and the city disappeared behind us. We made our way along a darker road to reach the castle where the wedding reception would be held.

The historic edifice appeared as we rounded a curve,

the stone façade shining under golden lights. Vicente had spared no expense on this sham of a wedding, inviting hundreds of people to witness his defiling of a young, unwilling girl. The ostentatious display was disgusting, but everyone in attendance seemed to think it was a joyous occasion.

The limo slowed to a stop, and Hugo ushered me out of the car. We stepped onto a red carpet, which led us through the open, massive wooden doors. More golden light spilled out into the night, welcoming us with false cheer. Marble floors shined under the massive crystal chandelier that lit the foyer.

Hugo wrapped his arm around my waist, but I stepped away as my stomach lurched. Over the years, I'd become numb to his touch. Tonight, it made my skin crawl. The memories of my own wedding night threatened to bubble up, and bile rose in my throat.

"Excuse me," I murmured. I couldn't come up with a good reason to leave Hugo's side, and I knew I'd pay for abandoning him later.

But all I could think about was fleeing from his slimy touch and rank scent.

I moved too quickly as I headed for the stairs, seeking privacy on the second level of the castle. No guests lingered around the banister on the upper floor, and I darted for the solace of a quiet room, where I could break down without witnesses.

The only thing worse than leaving Hugo standing alone in the foyer would be making a public scene. He'd be able to shrug off my sudden absence as the result of illness—I was sure I'd appeared pinched and pale enough in the limo to warrant that excuse.

No matter if the guests accepted his reasoning, he wouldn't allow me to go unpunished.

I could only hope that he'd wait until we were back on our estate. It was the most likely scenario. He wouldn't want to leave marks on me at this garish event; above all, he wanted others to believe that I truly was his devoted, loving wife. Anything less would be humiliating.

The second most powerful man in Bogotá couldn't have a disobedient wife. Hugo had made sure to break me and turn me into his adoring spouse a long time ago.

That had been after Adrián left me.

The boy I loved had left Colombia, and he'd never come back. He let Hugo torment me and turn me into his perfectly polished, soulless plaything.

Now, Adrián lurked downstairs with the rest of the sharks. The man who'd glowered at me in the church might wear the boy's face, but he wasn't here to rescue me.

I'd given up on that foolish fantasy a long time ago, anyway.

I slipped into the first open room I found, closing the door behind me. Books lined the walls, gold lettering gleaming on darkly colored spines. The unique scent of leather-bound books helped calm me. The library on Hugo's estate was the place where I most often found solace from him, losing myself in fiction for hours. I took a deep breath, inhaling the familiar smell. It helped calm my nerves and my nausea.

The door clicked open behind me, and I spun with a shocked yelp.

"What the fuck do you think you're doing?" Hugo's ruddy cheeks were redder than usual, almost purple with rage.

I took a hasty step back, raising my hands to ward him off.

Surely, he wouldn't strike me. Not here. Not now.

I hadn't prepared myself for the pain of his fists yet.

He slammed the door shut behind him, advancing on me. I backed up farther, until my butt hit the desk behind me. He leaned over me, pressing his hips against mine to pin me in place.

"I'm sorry," I squeaked. "I'm not feeling well."

"I don't give a fuck how you're feeling." His spittle hit my cheek, and I cringed away. "You think you can embarrass me in front of all our guests?"

I shook my head wildly. "I didn't mean to. I'm sorry," I repeated, desperate.

He leaned closer, so I could feel his putrid breath on my face. "I should bend you over this desk and fuck you raw." His cock jerked against my thigh as his cruel arousal rose along with his violence. "But I'd rather not have anyone hear you scream. You want to show me how sorry you are?"

I nodded frantically. "Yes. I really am sorry."

He stepped back. "Get on your knees. You know what to do."

The sick feeling in my gut intensified, my stomach churning. I sank to my knees, playing the part of obedient wife.

He quickly freed his cock from his slacks. It jutted toward my face, seeking the reluctant heat of my mouth.

I swallowed against the tang of bile on my tongue.

"Suck it," he seethed. "Show me you're sorry, and I won't beat the shit out of you when we get home."

Tears stung at the corners of my eyes as humiliation washed over me. I blinked them back. I wouldn't cry for him.

"Now," he snarled, thrusting his hips toward my lips.

I turned my face in revulsion, and his pre-cum wet my cheek.

He gripped my jaw, holding my head steady. "You'll pay for that later."

The door to the library opened, and my shame spiked. I couldn't bear to have anyone witness my degradation.

A fierce growl filled the room, and Hugo was ripped away from me. I watched in dumbstruck silence as Adrián tackled him to the floor. His massive fist connected with Hugo's jaw. My husband's head snapped to the side, blood spraying from his lips. Adrián didn't stop. He pummeled Hugo's face repeatedly, until crimson coated his knuckles and Hugo went completely still.

For a few long seconds, Adrián loomed over him, breathing hard. His lips peeled back from his teeth in a silent snarl, and his dark hair fell around his angular face, no longer arranged in its meticulous style.

Finally, he pushed to his feet and turned to me. He towered over me where I remained on my knees, frozen in place by shock at the sudden, violent display. His pale green eyes burned into me, and another feral sound slipped between his clenched teeth.

He reached for me with bloody hands. I shrank back, but that didn't deter him. His long fingers sank into my upper arms, yanking me to my feet.

He glowered at me for a moment, saying nothing. I shuddered in his grip, but I didn't dare struggle against him. I'd learned a long time ago that struggling only earned me more pain.

Hugo groaned, stirring at our feet.

Adrián's jaw ticked, but his shoulders relaxed, as though a decision had settled over him.

His grip shifted to my waist, and I shrieked as he tossed me over his shoulder.

His hand firmed on my upper thigh, squeezing hard enough to leave a mark. "Don't fight me," he ground out.

"What are you doing?" I asked, my voice shaking as fear suffused my system.

"I'm taking you."

ALSO BY JULIA SYKES

The Impossible Series

Impossible

Savior

Rogue

Knight

Mentor

Master

King

A Decadent Christmas (An Impossible Series Christmas Special)

Czar

Crusader

Prey (An Impossible Series Short Story)

Highlander

Decadent Knights (An Impossible Series Short Story)

Centurion

Dex

Hero

Wedding Knight (An Impossible Series Short Story)

Happily Ever After (An Impossible Series Christmas Special)

Valentines at Dusk (An Impossible Series Short Story)

Nice & Naughty (An Impossible Series Christmas Special)

The Subversive Series

Dark Lessons

The Stolen Series

Sweet Captivity

Claiming My Sweet Captive

Stolen Innocence

Stealing Beauty

The RENEGADE Series

RENEGADE: The Complete Series

The Daddy and The Dom

Dark Grove Plantation: Box Set

Wounded Hearts Duet

Wounded Hearts

Mended Hearts